Journey

to

Igniting

Dr. Monique Graves-Galloway

PURPOSEFUL
PUBLISHING & CONSULTING

LaTracey Copeland Hughes

CONTENTS

DEDICATION

THIS BOOK IS DEDICATED TO ALL THE WOMEN
WHO HAVE FELT AT ONE POINT IN THEIR LIVES.
YOU NO LONGER HAVE TO SUFFER IN SILENCE
WHILE ON YOUR JOURNEY.
WE SUPPORT YOU!!!

ACKNOWLEDGMENTS

TO ALL THE WOMAN THAT ARE EMBRACING
THEIR JOURNEY TO IGNITING. REMEMBER YOU
ARE NOT ALONE.
WE HAVE YOUR BACK!!!

Journey to

Igniting

Compiled by

LaTracey Copeland Hughes

Chapter 1

Chasing the bus

BEEEPPPPPP....The sound of the alarm that goes off and I wake up to the chirping of the birds. I push snooze 17 times before I finally get up because I dread the same path that I am taking daily. I chose this path as a sacrifice to allow my children to attend a school that masked the success that we often wear daily.

The routine of getting up, preparing for a day that I

regretted before it even arrived, just to please others. Ugh...sighing through the deep exhales in the shower only to see the Pantene bottle. On the bottle it says,' PowerFULL, flexible, high-intensity strength, natural fullness, full & strong,' and I am reminded that no matter what happens today God has equipped me with it!

Although equip, I get weary at times and the routine of waking up to put on the same mask day in and day out results in the delusion of the possibilities. Yet the chasing the bus seems to become a norm. From the outside looking in, people think that I have it all together. I make broken pieces look beautiful as the mosaic of my life's situation appears stunning. I suffered in silence as I try my best to please other people in the process only to see the bus pass me again.

Today was really difficult but I found peace in the message on Pantene bottle. The label said, "PowerFULL, flexible, high-intensity strength, natural fullness, full & strong". I had to ask myself, "What label am I carrying around that people see?" Am I really PowerFULL, flexible, high intensity of strength, natural fullness, full & strong? Do I display this even when I am running late, kids acting out, child support never arriving, bills are due and clients aren't paying for their services?

I cried at the thought that I didn't show those attributes to others because I was too busy "chasing the bus" to a destination unknown yet unfulfilling. Daily I question God on why am I on this journey to igniting? When will this assignment be complete? Who am I supposed to impact while on this journey? Will I ever receive my reward? Why won't these men stand up and be fathers to their daughters? Why can't I be loved like Christ loved the church? Where is the husband that you've chosen for me instead of the ones I picked to satisfy a thirst that only you can quench?

See while I building my successful business, Married yet single I was raising my children, and chasing the bus on the journey to igniting; I yearned for more while all these questions I waited to have them answered.

Yes...All these questions and the only answer I received was it for you! YES, YOU!!! The one reading this chapter and the one who sits up at night crying, hoping, wishing and praying for some answers.

I found the harmony in knowing that the same vehicle that I was brought in on for this assignment was a YELLOW Penske truck and now I am chasing a YELLOW bus. Yellow is uplifting and illuminating, offering hope, happiness, cheerfulness, and fun.

Seven years ago, God told me at one of my most vulnerable times to move from the high place to a lower ground. Minnesota was a location full of opportunity and advancement yet the cloud of doubt, discouragement, and despair kept me from receiving all that God had for me.

Once arriving in Mississippi, you can't get any lower than that in the United States, as a pioneer and temporarily settle in this unknown land to fulfill the assignment that was given to me. I've experienced loneliness, abandonment, and discouragement while traveling the path in front of me.

Dang, I find myself chasing this bus once again! Yet the journey ultimately was uplifting and illuminating, offering hope, happiness, cheerfulness, and fun. I just didn't recognize it while chasing the bus the reality of what was in front of me.

I see you are wondering how this journey can have both its highs and lows? Well, I decided that I am the only one who can determine the outcome of what is thrown at me. So, I made the choice to embrace this journey to igniting as God is the author and the finisher of my faith. I have a lot of faith. Faith makes things possible not always easy!

Crap, I am chasing this bus again!

The struggle is real, to say the least as I move forward on this journey to igniting. To chase an object that is the vehicle needed for me to move from where I am to where I am going!

I know what God told me and I believe it but who would have thought that the years of tears, disorganized mornings, illnesses, unpaid leave, unsafe environments, and unfulfilling days, overworked and underpaid would result in an elevation.

You see this morning I found myself chasing the bus one again but I caught it. I caught it because I knew that no matter the outcome was I WIN! I saw that the obstacles were being thrown at me like boulders in areas that would leave a lifetime of scars. But you see my scars are healing on the outside while scabbing up and leaving visible blemishes of the experiences that I once lived. So, this morning when I woke up before my alarm clock to see the sun peeping through my blinds I know that the effects of the journey weren't as traumatizing as I thought.

This journey to igniting included me chasing the bus but it wasn't the final destination as pioneers never settle. I will continue to write my way to healing and the results of it will lead me to birth purpose.

AUTOBIOGRAPHY OF

LATRACEY COPELAND

HUGHES

It's hard to sit on your talents, retreat from your destiny or settle for a less than optimized life when there's a spur in your side goading you to excellence. Blazing Empowerment Speaker, Best Selling Author and Publisher, La Tracey Copeland Hughes, also known as the Purposeful DIVA, has been that spur in the sides of countless audience members through her works, she encourages and motivates others to excel, kick off shackles and live abundantly by overcoming adversity and casting off a faltered start.

La Tracey Copeland Hughes' powerful ministry is for Kingdom-Minded entrepreneurs to be equipped and empowered to lead well in the marketplace. With her global voice, she is igniting the fire of purpose within them as they walk out their God-given assignments. La Tracey Copeland Hughes currently lives on the Mississippi Gulf Coast with her four children, Azuria,

Isaiah, Razaria, and Purpose.

Email: Latracey@latraceycopeland.com

Twitter:

www.twitter.com/ignitingfire

www.twitter.com/purposefuldiva

Website(s):

www.ignitingthefire.co

www.capstoneexperience.org

www.purposefulpublishing.org

Lesley Roberts

Chapter 2

5-4-3-2-1 Launch-Wait! Nothing is happening! 5-4-3-2-1 Launch-Wait! What is wrong with me? I can see the path. I know the destination, but why are all my systems stalling?

As a single mother of 2, from day one I made it my mission to give my children all the best of what I have to offer them of myself. Setting all my needs aside because their fathers were too selfish to give them any part of themselves. I was determined to give them the words I never had growing up; stability, protection, boundaries, selflessness, parenting, and Jesus. No disrespect to my own parents, but I can only speak from my perspective. I figured I would do for them what I felt like I needed.

So I worked. I had always kept a steady job for the most part. My children were never hungry, clothes were always clean, a roof over their heads, light bills were always paid, and they had every new toy or game imaginable. I had help from my aunt and uncle; who loved them as much as I did and was always there to pick up the slack. As my children became older, my parents became more present and also picked up some of the slack. On the side, I picked up photography and graphic designing. These were talents from God who allowed me to make extra money even to this day. I worked extra hard. Not for myself, but for my children. I had to prove to people like my parents, my children's fathers, and their family that I could make it without them. So, I bought a house, I had 2 cars, my children wore the best clothes, and I was present in their lives. I became full of pride. This was because I was still angry at all of them.

I got to a place in my life where I would rather suffer than ask for help. This was due to times in the past where I had received help, but it would always be thrown back into my face. So, if food got low, I would send my children to my aunt and uncle's house for the weekend. This was to ensure they would be fed. As for myself, I would eat the little of what we had until I figured out something. But make no mistake, I wasn't going to ask for anything from anyone. There was an incident where I didn't figure out anything and it was time to pick up my children. As they were packing their things, I went into my aunt's refrigerator and stole an entire roast. My pride would not allow me to ask for it nor tell my aunt we did not have food for the week. She would always back 2 or 3 bags of snacks for them to take home with them, but

God showed her that I need groceries. She began to unload her shelves and refrigerator of food into bags. She never knew I took the roast too.

Now that my children are grown, I felt like it was my turn to really launch (I have had businesses before, but lost my passion to continue and stopped pursuing them). I began searching for myself (Lesley). I realized that I did not know who the woman in the mirror was. I started on a quest to excavate myself. I started with pride. Learning to ask for help and to be okay with rejection (that only meant God did not want me in that particular place). This was a very painful process. I began to forgive my children's fathers. I began to forgive those who turned my life into their gossip. I began to forgive my parents. And finally, I forgave myself. Why forgive me? I was keeping people at bay from loving me; like those who had honest and true intentions to bless me. I chose toxic relationships that were ravaged by disappointments. I had no vision for my future. I figured out that I was only existing. Hiding behind the smiles I gave my children; telling them they can do and be anything. I was really telling them the things I was never told.

Because they had been affirmed their entire lives, one has graduated college and is looking for a job in his field, and the other is going to college to be a veterinary surgeon. The beautiful thing is, I have never shared this with my children. But they have always supported me and I affirmed me as a mother. Now that I am building my rocket to orbit around the world, they have started affirming me as a businesswoman as well. I found a declaration one of my children wrote about me. It says, "I am going to see my mother make tons of money in her business". I receive that.

I connected with God's plan for me, and I am where I

need to be at the right time.

"Hi. My name is Lesley Roberts, and I am a hurt and bitter person made whole."

5-4-3-2-1 Wait! Wait! Wait! I have it all together, I have forgiven others, my children support me, what now? For a short season, I was tired and emotional. It didn't feel physical, but it felt more spiritual. I would be literally exhausted after fussing at my children. My eldest child (as smart and talented as he is), dealt with fear and anxiety. When he would become overwhelmed, his skin would dry in rashes (eczema) in large patches. This also caused little self-conscious issues to top it off.

He went through a dark time where I could see the attacks from the enemy coming. So I began to fight for my child. Once, in church service, a prophet called him up and began to rebuke the spirits of suicide, oppression, and terror off of him. This is what I had been warring against, so you know I lost it. God showed up. As time would pass, and he would be okay, I was still feeling drained. I began to seek the Lord again and I was reminded that God had told me that he would take care of my son. God also revealed to me that it was my actions that was causing me to feel this way. I would get onto my son all the time about being immature, not taking the risk, and not taking responsibility for his life. So when he would do something for himself, I would always take the task away from him and do it for him. Registering for school, resumes, job hunting, and so on. He would let me do it because I had always done it throughout his entire life. I didn't want people to see him fail. I felt like if I did all these things for him, I would be protecting him. But God said it was hindering him. I was not allowing a God to teach and mature him.

Once I got that rebuked by the Lord, I had to repent. We all (my children and I) sat at the dining room table, and as tears began to roll down my face, I started apologizing to him and gave the explanation for the tears. We began to pray. I felt like I needed to release him to God and release all of the control issues that came along with it. I prayed "Father, I release all of my control and fear. I release my son back to you." Simultaneously, my son and I felt that spiritual release! The weight came off my shoulders and he felt like a rope had untied him from the waist. Now, he makes better decisions. He's happier and so am I.

5-4-3-2-1 I have to lift off! I have started my vision coaching business. I have connected with some awesome business people and God has really opened doors. I am walking for my purpose.

Autobiography

for

Leslie Roberts

L. Roberts is a confident and delightful single mother, professional graphic designer and photographer. Working closely with small businesses and nonprofit organizations to produce marketing and branding material, she found it very satisfying when consulting with new business owners about their vision for their businesses. As a result, she began her own coaching business. "Vision Unlocked". She is now on the road to making her vision a true reality.

L. Roberts

LRoberts@visionunlocked.com

678-421-4882

Nannette

Norvel

Chapter 3

The trails of life that we often walk seem unfair. Sometimes it's hard to bear the weight of the struggle and maintain a fulfilling life. In the course of this short dialogue, I will share my experience of how I overcame the impossible, reached for the unreachable, and achieved the unthinkable. I am Nannette and hereafter after I will be known as Felicia Jordan. I hope that you will enjoy this journey to igniting with me and we reach our goals and greatest potential.

Oh, how the simple things in life can become so complex. Whatever happened to the natural joys of life that bring what we call happiness, wholeness, love, devotion, and truth?

Did they forget about us?

The experiences of life were meant to strengthen us and help others. Often we may wonder why is it that the strength and knowledge gained from pain come from the very ones that we may have trust in our love? If you have never had your life disrupted this may not be for you. If at any time the truth you knew turned out to be lies allow me to help you in this walk.

Some of these seemingly constant cycles are not because of what we are but because of who we are. We are vessels of honor, dignity, virtue, love, compassion, understanding, truth, and integrity. We want to give chances and believe in others how we would want someone to believe in us. Do we always receive any of what all we give?

The natural born giver does not want to see anyone go without. The giver wants to be there to help. Often we put ourselves on the back burner considering the needs of others to be more important than our own needs.

Having this amount of love for people generally opens

us up for all that comes. Some of our giving are out of a pure heart and the rest is because we feel the need. The level of compassion has a lot to do with our love forgiving. Some of our utilities have been disconnected as a result of helping others.

Over the years two of my biggest issues the love and compassion that I observed and had not received from family, friends, and spouses was the same love that I constantly shared expecting that one day someone really would recognize that I deserve to be shown love and to be loved. Time after time I would get myself into situations because I was searching for love in all the wrong places and trying to fill voids in all the right areas.

Because of my childhood, which is a long story for another book, I didn't know what true love was, I didn't know what to look for, what not to accept as love, and how it should feel. I would hear people make the comment "love hurts" and seeing people in relationships fighting leaving knots and bruises. No, this is not loving. To hear women say "at least I have a man" and to see his disloyalty toward her and their children nope, I thought, that does not love either. To see male figures living in the home not working or providing while the woman is working and taking care of everything is not loved either.

I witnessed women excited about being a stay at home mom while the male was the breadwinner. The women had no free thought, authority, or dealings with the outside world. So now when he rants and she gets disgusted enough to want to leave guess what? She can't. She has distanced her from family, friends, associates and she possibly is under so much control she can't even look at or speak to the Male clerks in attendance out at the various stores. No, this is not loving. Some women are content and stuck on right now that she is satisfied with food, shelter and occasional events outside the home. This my dear does not love.

Of the many masks and facades that I have witnessed, I would always get this feeling that something was not right. Where is the fun, the freedom, the desire to want more? Why is this or these types of lifestyles so acceptable to some? Then I realized that some people were raised to believe that this was OK. The "A man is better than no man" mentality.

Walking the area that I was in at the time, I found myself observing, gaining knowledge, questioning and sometimes getting answers. What is real love?

Love covers a multitude of fault and error but love does not hurt, control or cause discord. So why settle for what we have seen or have experienced in previous moments of our lives by ignoring the signs that say RUN?

I guess you may be wondering about the compassion. Well, the compassion for helping or wanting to help someone can sometimes get us into trouble especially seeing that the person we are showing compassion to isn't always as receptive as we would hope. Especially when our concern is from the heart and not to for self-pride or to be seen; avoiding the spotlight.

Compassion has to come straight from the heart. Thinking of others and their needs minus greed is positive but on the flip side self-preservation, the first law of nature is when compassion will sometimes leave you in the dark. Uninformed compassion can be more painful than informed compassion.

With uninformed compassion, you can produce mind wrecking thoughts that you begin to feel used but actually, you have not been used. You were just uninformed. When you learn about wordplay manipulation and how these two components can come together and cause confusion, it will allow you to learn the importance of patience within compassion. Informed compassion will illuminate a lot of unnecessary pain and hurt if the receiving party is willing to be aided in the way that is deemed necessary if not move on no love lost. We can't help or save everybody and seasons of being used or taken advantage of are done and over with.

I can now say that I have grown in these areas simply by taking time to step back, look, listen, observe, pay attention to the times when I was in need and I had no one. I had to learn to save myself and love myself so that I could be there for myself. Don't dishonor or discredit love and compassion. If you can love yourself you can love someone else. If you can provide for yourself fulfill the need to take care of self. It is so much greater than the need to take care of another. I have a passion for the less fortunate especially the homeless but if I don't properly govern my life's happenstances properly then how can I be of help to anyone else?

In love I had to learn to love myself and prioritize situations events activities for myself no longer will I work to pay bills no longer will I sacrifice my life to assist The one who is draining the very life out of me I had to once again step back look, observe and pay attention to learn that no one on this earth will love me like me.

○ How has uniformed compassion hindered you?

○ How had informed compassion assist you in making better judgments

○ What has love taught you

Missing Nannette's Autobiography

Finding

Your

Greatness

Dr. Monique Graves- Galloway Ph.D.

Monique Galloway ©2017

Get ready to uncover these key strategies that will help you to not only unlock your potential but unlock the greater you!

Each of us is great. In each of us is greatness. In order to tap into your personal greatness, you have to be prepared to make a conscious effort to enable and empower that greatness. When you finally make the decision to seek out the greatness that is within you, you need to be prepared to put forth the required effort and hard work. After all, anything worth having is worth working for right? Exactly! So how do you become the greatest version of yourself? Let's dive in!

DEDICATION

I want to dedicate this work to my parents Willis and Mary Helen Graves. They both have been instrumental in helping me to understand the greatness that I have inside of me. God thought enough of me to allow these two blessings to raise me into womanhood. I am forever grateful. I love you both for LIFE.

G.R.E.A.T.N.E.S.S.

You are Great. During our day to day lives, we sometimes become stagnant. We think that what we do every day is what we need to do for the rest of our lives. We often work 9-5 jobs, come home, cook dinner, see that the kids have what they need, make sure our husbands and wives are good, take a shower, go to bed, get up in the morning and do it all over again. Whew! That was long sentence! Just from that sentence we see that many of us, once we get home from work, have to make sure that everything and everyone except ourselves is happy and content. In the meantime, we still have dreams and aspirations that we want to pursue but often talk ourselves out of it because we are overwhelmed with everything and everybody. We unconsciously forfeit our dreams and goals because our focus is on everything except ourselves. Now don't get me wrong, it is important that we take care of our families and keep steady employment to keep a roof over our heads. However, if there was no you, how would these things get done? You guessed it. They wouldn't. If you were to disappear into thin air as if you never existed, life as we know it has to progress and move on. So what happens to that fire inside of you that wanted to grow into something great? Nothing. Absolutely nothing. Remember, if you no longer exist, then that fire inside of you ceases to exist as well. One thing that we as individuals in this big universe have to remember is that we have the ability to change our own reality. We have the ability to change our lives. That fire that I mentioned, we have the ability to IGNITE it! How do you ask? By realizing that we are Great.

According to Merriam-Webster's dictionary (2017), the definition of great varies when being used as an adjective, noun or adverb. As an adjective, Merriam-Webster (2017) defines great as "of an extent, amount, or intensity considerably above the normal average." Additionally, Merriam-Webster (2017) continues to define great as "of ability, quality, or eminence considerably above the normal average." As a noun, Merriam- Webster (2017) defines great as "a great or distinguished person". Lastly, as an adverb great is described by Merriam- Webster (2017) as "excellently very well." So what does all of this mean? It means that you as an individual are more than average. It means you as an individual have abilities that are above normal and above average. It means you as an individual are a great and distinguished person. It means you as a child of God is…. excellent. When you change the way you think about yourself and allow yourself to nurture and release the greatness that you have inside of you, your entire world will change. Remember that fire inside of you that I mentioned earlier in the text, it's time to IGNITE it!

RESILIENT

You are Resilient. Romans 8:37 says "no, in all things we are more than conquerors through him who loved us". Fear and rejection often hold us back from reaching our full potential. But if the Bible says that we are more than conquerors, then we have the potential to conquer anything. Yes, many of us have failed at something at some point in our lives, but we have the ability to pick ourselves up and reinvent ourselves over and over until we get it right. We are resilient and we can conquer anything. Change how you see yourself and change your mindset. In order to allow yourself to become the greatest version of yourself, you have to strip all of the layers that are holding you back. These layers could be relationships, people's opinions of us, even our surroundings. We don't have control of what people's opinions of us are. Their opinions will change but how you see yourself will stand. In the end, it's just you as an individual in this big universe that is holding vast opportunities just for you. We need to find the tools that we need to work this. Can you become greater? Are you existing to your full potential? Don't be afraid to tap into it. Your perception will change and you will open yourself up to infinite possibilities. We all can have these things. It's not just for certain people like the friend that is so successful and everything that she touches turns to gold. It's not just for the guy from our church that is a successful entrepreneur and every day he seems to become more and more successful. It's for you too! There is more than enough to go around. We can have a piece of the pie too. And guess what, there is a piece of pie with your name on it! When your body, mind, and spirit are interconnected, you begin to visualize the magnificence inside of you. Be alive and LIVE! Clear negative energy and be free. Never get so caught up in the outcome that you miss the process. You can only become your greatest self and tap into your greatness when you love yourself as well as the process. Many of us on our journey think about things that no longer serve us. We have to take 100 percent responsibility for our current conditions. No one is doing anything to us. The secret to becoming greater is not to externalize your power. Many of us take too much time thinking about someone that drains our energy. We have to think about people who inspire us and love us. Stop thinking about things or someone that we do not resonate with. We have to let go of our fear and stop living in the mind and start living in our heart. The heart does not know fear unless we think about it. Whatever you focus on, you give energy to. This is one of the secrets to becoming the greatest version of yourself. Focus on what elevates you because what you focus on grows. We have to let go of society's expectations because, in the end, you cannot please everyone. Live from your heart and be yourself instead of a poor version of someone else. Are you eating to live or eating to die? Become greater, go into nature, listen to beautiful music, share yourself with other people and learn to connect with fellow kindred spirits. Who are you sharing your visions and dreams with? If that person does not have your best interest at heart, they will steal and literally attempt to destroy your dream. Push yourself to the limit and then you will realize that there is no limit except the limit that you create with your own mind. Place a sign in your window that says "No Energy

Vampires Allowed". Once you change your mind and the way you think, you begin to change your world. When your world begins to change, that fire that I mentioned earlier will begin to grow larger. Is that the fire inside of you waiting to IGNITE? Let's examine this a little further.

EVOLVING

You are always Evolving. As you begin to uncover, layer by layer the greatness that is inside of you screaming to come out, you begin to evolve. You begin to undergo changes and develop your own way of seeing and perceiving the world. Now is the time that you open your eyes and awake to the infinite possibilities that await you. By now, you probably have had many people tell you that "you can't do this" or "it will never work." You may have even been told that you will never succeed in life because of one reason or another. But now, as your mind evolves and you become more in tune with who you are, you begin to realize that no one has the power to strip you of who you are. No one has the power to make you feel inferior. The power is within you to make your own reality. Travel to a place you have never been before, open your mind and do not live closed off to the world around you. You have to free yourself from who you thought you were before you began this journey. Anything that is putting you in a box, get rid of it. Break free from it. Update your internal system. When we have new and updated information within, our internal system is able to work more efficiently. We are living in a world of distraction. We are programmed by people, television and media outlets feeding us information on a daily basis that is placing so much negative energy in our systems that we lose sight of who we are and what we want to accomplish in this life. We lose sight of the overall purpose of our existence. In order to get your internal systems back in working condition, you have to place yourself in the right environment. For example, flowers need to be in the right environment where sunlight and water are plentiful so that they may grow. We as individuals need to be in the right environment where we can grow and evolve. The right environment is vital to have as we grow into our passions and our purpose. Everything that we have to give to this world, is waiting to be awakened. Proverbs 18:16 says that "a man's gift makes room for him and brings him before great men." This is the time to clear out and update your system so that your gift has a rich environment to flourish, evolve and grow. As your journey continues, you begin to evolve and the fire within you is awaiting that spark to IGNITE it! Now is the time to enlarge your territory! Let's go!

ABUNDANCE

You exist in Abundance. You live in a world full of infinite possibilities. Let's take a stroll down memory lane. Do you remember when you were a young child, just learning to crawl or walk? During this time, you were a small vessel just ready to explore the world. Everything that you saw with your eyes, you wanted to explore and find out what it was. It may have been your mothers' shoe or you sisters' car keys. It may have been a spoon or all of the pots and pans in the cabinet. It may have been a pencil or pen, even a piece of paper or a book. Whatever it was, you would grasp it in your hand, put it in your mouth, pick it up and shake it just to hear the sound that it would make. Everything that your eyes saw you wanted to explore it. This was a time when you were a tiny person in this world full of things that were all around you. This was your personal playground of things. Different color things. Different shaped things. Things that made different sounds when you would manipulate them. Right? Now let's fast forward to now. Now you are an adult, still in this same world of things but now you feel that you are in this big world and none of these things are within your grasp. You constantly say that you don't have the things you want or need. It seems that everyone around you has a surplus of things and you don't. Things like houses, cars, successful careers and money. Right? Well, here is where you are wrong. You see, when you begin to visualize the greatness that you possess, you begin to understand that you have the power to manifest the reality that you want. Romans 4:17 says "As it is written: I have you the father of many nations. He believed in God, who gives life to the dead and calls things into existence that do not exist." The tongue has power and you have the power to speak what you want your reality to be. Speak it! Shout it! Whether it may be a successful career or that book that you have been wanting to write. Speak it until you begin to see the words that you have spoken. Speak to the new house, speak to the sold-out crowds at your next event, speak to the new car or speak to that college degree. Learn to become awake and speak to the universe that you live in abundance already! You live in a world of infinite possibilities. All of these things are here and they are waiting for you. You have to believe in your heart that it is possible to get the things that you want within the abundance of things of this universe. Put forth the effort to work for the things that you want. Grab and pen and write it down. Set both short term and long term goals for yourself. Be resilient. Evolve. Go out and get it! It's yours for the taking! All you need is a tiny little spark to IGNITE that fire. You are that spark. Are you ready yet?

TREASURE

You are Treasure. You are a special gift of life that cannot be replaced with anything else. You are a one of a kind gem that cannot be duplicated. Each one of us has unique DNA that sets us apart from everyone else on this planet. When you were born, in a random combination, half the DNA came from your mother and half of your DNA came from your father. Now here is where it gets amazing! Even though everyone has different DNA, you share around 99.9% of your DNA with everyone else. Actually, there is only a 0.01% difference between you and everyone else in the world. Due to the fact that we have such a large amount of DNA, that 0.01% difference is actually a lot. Taking into consideration, that such a small amount of DNA sets us apart from everyone else on the planet proves two things. First, we are all connected as beings in this universe and secondly, we all possess DNA and genes that are passed down to us from our parents that gives us individual traits. Several philosophers before us believed that all of the creation is actually one. Whether you call where we live our world, the material universe, matter or energy, the fact is that we are all just tiny particles of something bigger than we are. Some believe that we are just tiny droplets in this big universal ocean and therefore we are all connected in some way. Our own individual consciousness are all a part of a bigger consciousness which is God. By being connected to one another we can also influence one another. We can affect one another in both positive and negative ways. That's why we should always be aware of what we think in our minds and what we say out of our mouths to others. When we send positive emotions out to others in this world, we will receive positive emotions back. When we think of ourselves as treasures, it becomes easy for us to think of others the same way. When we treat ourselves as treasures, it becomes easy for us to treat others in the same manner. Thinking positive thoughts about yourself will manifest those same positive thoughts about others. When you see a person, pretend that they are a mirror of yourself. When you smile at them, they will smile back. We are all beings, beings that are composed of energy. Everything around us is energy and we are connected to it in some way. We are all small particles of energy in this universe. We are a part of God. God is everywhere. And even in this big universe of particles, energy, and matter, we are treasures that cannot be duplicated. One of a kind gems is what we are. God created us all, different and unique for a reason. Treasure your greatness. By doing so you have nothing to lose but everything to gain.

NOTABLE

You are a Notable. According to Merriam-Webster's Dictionary (2017), the definition of notable is worthy of attention or remarkable. Let's read that out loud. The definition, according to Merriam- Webster's Dictionary (2017) is worthy of attention or remarkable. Here is where I have to take a pause for a minute because I want this to really sink in your mind. I began to practice the art of positive self-talk way before it was on every inspirational speakers' agenda. When you constantly live in a world of constant chaos, we often find ourselves feeling down, in the dumps, and depressed about things that we have no control over. When I learned and began to practice the art of positive self-talk, I was able to bring the positive out of any negative situation and it allowed me to discover that in every situation there is joy and there is hope. Then I begin to focus on me. One day while I was sitting in my room looking in the mirror, I said, "girl you are worthy and you are a remarkable person." I then went on to say, "Monique you are a notable person with a lot to give this world and God himself has preordained it to be so." I had no idea at the time, where those two statements came from. Like the words just formed on my lips and I began to say them. Now, looking back I realize that God was speaking to and through me. Matthew 10:20 says that "for it will not be you speaking, but the Spirit of your Father speaking through you." So, the next time that words form on your lips and they just come out of your mouth, remember that a higher power is speaking to and through you. You may not speak in tongues or even believe in it for that matter but one thing is for certain that when you ask God wholeheartedly to speak to you and through you, magical words will form on your lips, magical sounds will be in your ears, and belief will be in your heart that you are worthy of the love of God and you are remarkable in his image in every way.

EXTRAORDINARY

You are Extraordinary. This is one of my favorite words. A person who is extraordinary is, well, extraordinary. That person is very unusual or exceptional. I have been unusual all of my life. I have never really been one to try to be like anyone else. I have always had my unique perspective on the world. I also have had my own belief system. When I was a child, I remember my uncle Ralph (Rat) telling me that there is only one Mona. He called me Mona, which I loved to hear him say. But even in that statement, I understood that not only do I feel that I am unique but possibly others do too.

During my life, I have been talked about, disliked for no apparent reason, and even bullied in my early school days. Looking back on it now, we can say that it was just children being children but I do feel that it was more than that. You see, I was different and people often times are uncomfortable with different. They don't understand different and therefore it causes an unsettling feeling. At some point during the unsettling, anger and resentment develops and you have an innocent person being mocked and disliked for a really apparent reason. Now if I were to ask certain persons what was the reason for all of the anger towards me in those early years, they would probably say something like "we were just young and didn't know any better." Yea, ok. But do you want to know the real reason? Well, here it is. You see I was born an extraordinary person. I had my own uniqueness about myself. I liked what I liked and I never just went along with what the crowd of people who thought the same, acted the same, dressed the same and were the same, did. I looked at strangers as my sisters or my brothers. I could sense when people were hurting and when they needed just a kind word. I would give away my possessions, unbeknownst to my parents, to others because I wanted them to have just as much as I had. I wanted my friend who grew up without a father to be welcome in my home to talk to and be mentored by my dad. I wanted that friend who didn't have a mother figure to be welcome in my home to hear words of wisdom from my mom. I wanted to feed the hungry and clothe those in need. I wanted to speak life to everyone that I encountered. I was selfless and I cared more about other people than I cared about myself. I would stay up all night sometimes trying to find a way to help someone get out of a bad situation. I never really cared if they would ever bless me like I blessed them. I never understood why God made me that way. Why couldn't I just be selfish, egotistical and be liked by everyone? Why couldn't I just blend in with everyone? Why couldn't I be chosen as the Most Liked or Class President or The Most Likely to Succeed in one of those rigged class elections that take place in high school? This is the reason. I was born to stand out. How people felt or what people thought of me never defined who I was. God gave me the definition of me. He created me to be selfless. He created me to spread the love. He created me to help others and give the hopeless hope. He created me to give selflessly to others without asking anything in return. He created me to be Extraordinary! For that, I give him thanks. You are extraordinary too. Just believe it. Just say it. It is so.

STRONG

You are Strong. We were born with physical and mental strengths to handle the many obstacles that we will face in this life. Just face it, we were born this way. However, sometimes along the way we get mentally and physically defeated. Sometimes we just throw in the towel and say "I'm done." Well, let me tell you this, on your journey to greatness, there will be some good days and there will be some bad days. There will be molehills and there will be mountains. But, the good thing is that you can handle it. If you can train your mind to handle life's obstacles and take the David and Goliath approach, you will defeat your opponent every single time.

From the biblical context of the story of David and Goliath, David a shepherd, was the youngest of eight sons and King Saul and his army were engaged in combat with the Philistines. The Philistines secret weapon was a 9- foot giant named Goliath. Saul and his army were afraid of Goliath and they had no one that was willing to stand up for him. Goliath, who blasphemed

God's name and taunted his existence upset David and he stood up for God by standing up to Goliath. With only five stones, a sling and staff, David hurled a stone at the center of Goliath's forehead and defeated him...just like that. David went on to cut off Goliath's head with his own sword but we will just end the story right here.

Now what? Well, just by looking at this biblical account of courage, strength, and faith, you will see that David, small in stature as compared to Goliath, really didn't have a chance of defeating him considering his size. Goliath was challenging God's people by challenging them to show that their God was more powerful than him. But you see, David was willing to step out on faith and face Goliath. He had faith that was so strong that he was willing to believe that God would be with him and enable him to defeat this big giant that everyone was afraid of. From this story, you will see that when you believe that you can defeat whatever giant you face in life, you will succeed. Strength is something that we all possess, but faith compliments strength. A wise man once said that fear and faith cannot coexist. So you need to tap into the strength that you already have, sprinkle on lots of faith and you have a recipe for overcoming any situation that you are faced with. Go ahead, give it a try.

SELECTED

You are Selected. Here, when I say selected, I mean chosen. Chosen how a husband chooses a wife or how judges choose a person to win a contest. Well, have you ever wondered why you were selected by God to be born and be a part of this world? What was so special about you that God chose to create you to live the life that you currently live?

We can go to any bookstore and see hundreds and

thousands of books dedicated to telling you why you were created and the reason for you being here in this world. They even go so far as to tell you how to uncover your gifts or your anointing. People often will read the bible and search for the reasons why you were selected by God. However, some people still don't understand what they were selected to do exactly.

By reading the bible it leads you to a deeper understanding of the man that was called Jesus. However, you can read the bible in its entirety front to back, many times over, but if you don't enter into a personal relationship with God or a higher power than yourself, you will always be frustrated and feel unfulfilled. There are thousands of churches that teach you how to be something or how to do something but leave out one important thing that many people are still left confused about. What were you selected to do?

First, you were selected to be near God, have access to God and have an intimate relationship with God. The scriptures tell us throughout the Bible that God does not select us because he needs us, he selects us because he wants us. Remember that God lacks nothing. He selected us because he wanted to interact with us and be close to us. God does not want us to stand at a distance, he wants us to be close to him and commune with him. (Psalm 65:4, Psalm 84:10, Revelation 22:17). It is hard for many people to understand this because they have been rejected more often than they have been selected, but from the time you were in the womb of your mother (Psalm 139) God wanted you. God chose you. God selected you and from this day forward he will continue to select you over and over again. God chose you based on his limitless mercy and not your performance. You will never earn, deserve, work hard enough for or be perfect enough to amount to Gods selection of you. This, my friend, is what God, the creator of the universe selected you for. Now that you know that your selection was a divine selection from our creator, I want you to understand that it was not by chance. God selected you long before you selected him. You have the power to you to do whatever you want in this life. You are a part of God and he is a part of you. Who wouldn't want to be that close to something that powerful? You have been selected to experience joy and satisfaction and we are designed to find our satisfaction not from ourselves but from our creator. You were endowed with unique gifts and talents. Put your gifts to use and use them faithfully for they will be enlarged. Just let that sink in for a minute.

G.R.E.A.T.N.E.S.S.

Well, my friends, this is where my story ends. By now you have realized that each section of this work has been devoted to explaining to you that your greatness is inside of you just waiting for that extraordinary moment to be released! We all have these gifts that are given to us when we are born. These gifts can't be bought or sold. You can't trade your gift with someone else. It is yours. It was crafted and made especially for you. God created it and placed it inside of you. Ephesians 2:10 says that "for we are God's masterpiece. He has created us anew in Christ Jesus, so we can do the good things that he planned for us long ago.". With that being said, from this day forward, I want you to own your greatness. Why? Because it is yours! Wake up every morning expressing gratitude for things that you have and things that you don't. Give thanks for being able to be a part of the humanity of this world that was created for Gods glory.

Live your life on purpose. It is up to you to use your gift

and glorify God while doing it. Take time out to breathe

in the fresh air from the earth, taste the salt in the rain

and feel the wind on your face. Spread love and

compassion throughout the world regardless if it is

welcomed or not. Teach yourself to love who you are and

what you, as a tiny vessel, bring to this immense world

that we live in. We live in a world of vast opportunities

and those opportunities belong to you. Pay it forward,

and forward, and forward. Be a blessing to others in the

light and in the dark. Take that fire that you have within

and set it ABLAZE. The time is now for you to walk in

your greatness. No one on this earth can do it quite like

you can. Now, I challenge you to ask God to ignite your

fire. I challenge you to ask the universe to give you the

strength and spiritual power to walk into your greatness. I

challenge you to channel your God-given gift like only you know how to do. I challenge you to simply be that living masterpiece that God intentionally created you to be. Now go, the world is waiting.

With Love,

Dr. G

2017

Autobiography of

Dr. Monique D.

Graves- Galloway

Dr. Monique Graves- Galloway is an author, certified counselor, intellectual disabilities therapist, psychological assessment reviewer, grant writer, consultant, educator and co-owner of Labat Galloway LLC. Dr. Galloway has always thought that there was a higher purpose for her life. She grew up in the small town of Bassfield Mississippi and was the product of two educators, Professor Willis C. Graves and Mary Helen Graves who both instilled in her the purpose of education. She graduated a year early from Bassfield High School and she went on to study at William Carey University at the age of 16. She went on to earn her B.S. degree in Psychology, a Master's Degree in Counseling, a Specialist degree in Education and a Doctorate Degree in Higher Education Administration. During her adult years, she earned a certification in Gerontology and she has studied the field of Sociology. Dr. Galloway continues to be an advocate for children and adults with special needs, specifically children diagnosed with Dyslexia. Dr. Galloway currently lives in Hattiesburg, Mississippi and she is currently married to her husband Minister Jeris "Mark" Galloway and has twin boys Ace Pierre Galloway and Bentley Jackson Galloway. She has one sister, Rymsky Graves- Labat who is very successful in her own right.

Dr. Galloway has always been a different and unique individual. She was the one that would "think outside of the box." She had her own unique view of the world and this is what set her apart. Growing up in the church she was raised to acknowledge God. However, it was not until adulthood that she began to have a true spiritual relationship with God and then her eyes were truly opened to the wonders of the world. Now pieces of the puzzle that were missing in her life all came together, and they had to mean. It was through her search for a higher power and higher meaning in life that has brought her to this point in her life. Today she continues to empower others, gives selflessly for the betterment of her sisters and brothers and teaches others to learn to embrace who they are, tap into their potential and be the greatest version of themselves that they can be for the betterment of this world.

Email: counselorgalloway@gmail.com

Email: doctorgalloway601@gmail.com

Twitter: www.twitter.com/DrMonaG

Facebook: www.facebook.com/DrMonique Graves-Galloway (Dr. G)

Instagram: https://instagram.com/Dr. Mona G

Labat & Galloway LLC: P.O. Box 17286 Hattiesburg, MS 39404

Beatrice Moore

"The Journey To Igniting: (From The Inside, Out!)"

We all know that no measure of success happens overnight. It is a culmination of ingredients that can be conflicting, that work together to produce a product that many see, some celebrate and some, envy. The elements involved in becoming [anything] can either stand alone as a flawless reflection of who a person is or came from, or be converted by one decision to allow all things to work together for the good and to the glory of God! The decision to be; whether it having been an easy path, or a creative one of making messy spills into a life that is a work of art, speaks to who a person is and makes irrelevant the difference of where either person had begun. — I honor both sides of the successful person's journey! It takes courage, audacity and in some cases, tenacity to walk in God's promises for us! So as an offering to what is already an amazing book because of the authors who have contributed, here is my testimony and journey to igniting!

As the youngest of four siblings and the product of my mother's marriage to my father, it was almost inevitable. Who was really ready to accept a new addition to their lives? I was the child who was obviously different from the rest of the crew and was in some ways despised because of it. —I was the "happy girl" who loved her daddy; who brought home A's and 1's in citizenship in an environment that didn't offer much hope. We struggled to make ends meet and became innovative when desperate times, called for desperate measures. Having nothing of my own but my father's love in an environment where my one thing, wasn't everyone's abroad, meant a grief and for me an exclusion that I could in no way ignore. My world as a young girl was loud. I was consumed by the inaudible mourning of my sibling's hearts and the all too audible of my two unhappy parents. I needed either really good earplugs or a spirit that could go on vacay! — I needed a break!

Fast forwarding through years' worth of experiences, I'd begun to do my own "storing up" of the information I'd gathered through various moments and events in my adolescence into adulthood. Before launching out into my business, I had gone through a very dark and difficult season; one like I'd never experienced. It was hard. It was heavy. It was alone walk and because of what I know now, it was necessary as it was the threshold to entering into my life's callings.

Like a photo album, I can look back through the lies that I was infested with that had been adopted throughout my younger years starting back at home. Every lie that I could have ever imagined to have existed had finally made its way up to 'the mic' of my life and boy did it speak! I'd believed myself down to the place of self-hate and had allowed life to convince me that there was no use in doing good or for me, is good. The feelings of rejection have been so deeply engraved into my belief system after years of inwardly fighting for a place in life, I'd found myself finally accepted... in the arms of a [married] man who, whether he knew it or not, depended on every lie that I believed that would keep me that much more entangled in the sticky web of deception and susceptible to manipulation. The inner conflict between what I wanted to do and what I didn't want to do that I did, alongside the felt inability to talk about what I was dealing with was... —similar to the feeling that many of us growing up had maybe experienced in regards to dealing with issues outdoors that existed [inside] of our homes, and that was to not say anything because, as the saying goes "what happens at home, stays at home"! —

And so there I was, this gifted, intelligent, beautiful woman (who loved God) found in a place of being 'virtuously' imprisoned to the weight of unresolved issues that resulted in bad behavior all the while reliving this law to "keep quiet" to ultimately, avoid shame. This woman who once knew exactly who she was, because of these things, had come to a place of wondering... who she was anymore! It was this season and experience that would shift me to a desire that as long as I could help it, that no one would be found in this position again!

Somewhere between Truth that was the door to my destiny, and lies that would lead to my demise, I felt trapped in the foyer of two seasons; each holding, a needed version of me; One lesser (leaving) and another being birthed out of me! While living in the "cusp" of two seasons, I lived destructively in a way that could only be explained to have been an effort to break free of a mold that I was growing uncomfortable in! I lived agonized at the feel of "stitches breaking" as I began bursting at the seams with this 'potential'. This potential, oppressed and suppressed converted and became perverted at the reach for someone who I would later become who retrieving instead, would turn my power to do well into a weapon to [self] destruct.

"When the purpose is not known, abuse is inevitable"-

Dr. Myles Munroe

Because I'd never seen who I knew that I was to be in her rare form, nor had I the way to become it, merely feeling this greatness without a midwife to help me deliver this baby nearly drove me nuts! This 'untapped potential', alongside the lies that had now become tangible, had like a boa constrictor wrapped itself around me until life as I knew it; Living honestly, honorably, loving purely and wholeheartedly became bleak! — I

BLACKED OUT!

INVENTION

It was like an angel sat with me one afternoon over a cup of coffee and began to ask me who I was. I told him who I thought I might be as I trodden carefully not to confuse and allow who I'd become to interfere and taint my self-perception of who I knew that I really was. He seemed to already know a little bit about me; my interests, that I was a believer and that I had a gift to sing. (Thank God for Facebook!) With all mess on the table; my confession, my reality and everything else in between, he kindly suggested that I enroll into a school that he was affiliated with that offered a program for Christian Counseling. —My face, a little shocked that his first thought was that I would make for a good Christian - anything, immediately lit up!

See, the truth was, that years ago I'd dropped out of

college because I'd get discouraged because, after several

attempts, I could not pass a ridiculously hard math course

that I needed in order to graduate with my bachelors in

psychology; the subject that I LOVE! With everything

that had taken place up and to the moment of sitting

down to drink that cup of coffee with said "angel", I was

able to see and experience first-hand the need for a

[Christian] counselor! (Why not have the best of both

worlds operating at once?) The fact that he saw [me] and

not what I did, and went even a step further to fix my

train track so to speak, inspired me and caused me to feel

a lot less like a Casper the not-so-friendly ghost and more

alive like the Ayanna that I knew was still there! I knew

then that this would be the moment and decision that

would change my life!

It would only be after a few weeks after attending

classes that my eyes, like a newborn, would be made wide open! Words like, "codependency" lied everywhere! I could see everything and everyone like a clear glass of water and me there I stood, amazed!

SELF CHECK

(Song of Solomon 2:15) "Catch the foxes for us, the little foxes that spoil and ruin the vineyards, while our vineyards are in blossom."

Because the issue was not that I was "no good" or that I was incapable or didn't have the sense enough to 'Luh God' but was rather, that the truth [of Christ] and [His] thoughts about me had not yet filled up the foxholes that those little furry lies had dug! —They were still yet "running around" having a field day eating on the very fruit that I knew that my life had to offer but I could not see because they were all but pureed sitting in their bellies! Because if this, I birthed Ascended Volition, LLC (2016) a brand and business founded upon the Christian faith that provides both Counseling and Life Coaching services to individuals who are in need of healing, hope purpose and direction! Ascended Volition has also a clothing line that serves the believer through fashionable tees! In the same year, my first book, "Living From Fullness; Acting Empty (The Perfect Love Story For The Bruised) was launched to help readers to discover the internal roadblocks that hinder living in the fullness of who they are and who they are to be and later that year, my second book, "The Beasts Hidden In The Beauty Of Success" a book that coaches individuals through to experiencing the fulfillment of their life's purposes!

—I write this chapter as a testimony to you: All things can work together for the good and to the glory of God...

if you want it to! You do not have to have a "perfect storm" in order to have a purpose, you just have to have faith, the right perspective, Truth, wisdom and a willingness to change and become the best you! You may encounter those who, to keep you under or to bring you back to the life that you left, will try to bring to your attention things that God does not care about nor is He limited by or remind you of what is now irrelevant because of what you've chosen now to do; Keep forward! Believe! Take chances! Don't be moved by every voice that fights for your attention. Be careful who you share your dreams with! Those who lack faith and are controlled by fear will project their fear on you and will speak you right off of your path and destiny! When things are rough in the light, don't forget what was spoken to in the dark! Don't act according to where you are, work according to where you are going... and don't stop until you see what He said! And most importantly, value your hand in life! Whether you're privileged or not so privileged, once you begin to value your hand in life, you will begin to benefit from it... and so will those whom you are to reach!

From my heart to your dream...— You were made for greatness!

Autobiography of

Ayanna Mann

Ayanna Mann, born March 22, 1989 in the City of
Detroit, is the youngest of four siblings. While moving
frequently throughout her life as a result of her parent's
divorce, Metro Detroit had always been the place that she
has called "home". Despite facing many challenges prior
to reaching adulthood, she had established at an early in
age her foundation in God. Ayanna attends Destiny
School of Ministry where she studies Christian
counseling through CCI (Christian Counseling Institute)
specializing in inner healing. In 2016 Ayanna launched
her business, Ascended Volition, LLC which is a brand
and business geared to empower individuals and aid them
through life transitions. In 2016 Ayanna released her first
book, " Living From Fullness; Acting Empty" (The
Perfect Love Story For The Bruised) a book of inner
healing and later, her second book, "The Beasts Hidden
In The Beauty Of Success" a book geared to help

individuals to discover success for themselves. Ayanna has dedicated her life to helping individuals break free from internal strongholds and breakthrough to their potential by investing into the 'whole person' through both inner and outer change! Ayanna works to provide opportunities for individuals to become equipped and released to begin living fulfilled lives through her company.

While Ayanna offers her services to everyone, she offers spiritual counseling and spiritual life coaching to those who are of the Christian faith. Ayanna's desire through Ascended Volition LLC is to simply be the need met for those whom she serves by providing them both a sense of hope, purpose and direction!

Beatrice Moore

How I got Over-Prayers from a Woman on the Edge about to let go and then She Let God!

How I got Over- Prayers from a Woman on the Edge about to let go and then She Let God!

Yet, if you surrender to Him, obey Him and serve Him, God will become your loving Father, your Protector, your Healer, the Giver of "every good and perfect gift" (James 1:17) and the One who has abounding love and mercy. "For as the heavens are high above the earth, so great is His mercy toward those who fear Him; as far as the east is from the west, so far has He removed our transgressions from us. As a father pities his children, so the LORD pities those who fear Him. For He knows our frame; He remembers that we are dust" (Psalm 103:11–14).

I have always considered myself a believer. But I did not understand the full power of prayer until I found myself standing on the edge of life's cliff. I stood there transfixed. Wondering how to reach the other side without falling into the darkness that lay between my present and my future. And I have stood there many times. But by His grace and mercy, each time I journeyed there, I made it to the other side.

Death. Love. Depression. Guilt. Rejection. Perfection. Confusion. A short list of the cliffs at which I have stood. I always thought love by itself was enough. I wanted a blanket of love to protect me. I thought I could find someone to love me enough to protect everyone from everything. Wait, who was I looking for, Superman? Flying high, taking his blanket of love and transforming it into his cape. Sweeping me up in his arms so that I may fly above all these issues that haunted me. I could just envision flying high with my Superman. My tears of joy would shower like rain and just as in nature, erode away all those cliffs. And I did just that. My tears showered with the rain but that rain never fixed anything.

Sometimes they fell between loud claps of thunder as voices rose in disagreement. Other times, I cried out in pain not caring who heard and my tears were like a raging river, carrying anyone and anything near me to certain destruction. I cried as I consoled and empathized. And then there were those muffled tears, with my head in the pillow. I cried but did not want anyone to know my pain. I flew to those cliffs each time, solo. No Superman, just me and my tears. And each time I landed at the edge I came closer and closer to going over. Life was exhausting, my tears evaporated oh so quickly and I was learning that love alone was not enough. What I needed was the power of prayer combined with the love for my God to transform me into my own Superwoman self.

My story is not so unique. But my journey of self-examination and exploration was transformational. At each of these cliffs, I learned how the power of prayer protected, provided and guided me. Each cliff offered me the opportunity to fall or to fly. Because of these cliffs, I have developed the essential emotional, psychological and spiritual developmental that my loving God desired for me all along.

As I teetered at the cliff of self-esteem, I reflected on why I would not let go of the blame, shame, and guilt that fed my low-self-esteem and fueled my desire for perfection and acceptance. I needed to dig deep and see where this was rooted? How was it birthed in me? Low self-esteem lurked all around me. It was a shadow, not allowing me to shine as brightly as I was destined. I began to realize that my self-esteem was rooted in my lack of emotional progress. I was never "good enough," and in turn, I became an overachiever, a perfectionist by the time I was in college. I grew up in a busy household. I was not told by those closest to me that I was loved.

Rather, I was shown love through being provided for with the necessities and rewarded with occasional wants. At school, I was taught I had to compete to get noticed to receive. And because the demonstration of love was lacking I chose inappropriate relationships and people. This culminated in me becoming an unwed teen who was told over and over I would be nothing. I had messed up my life. I had a family who loved me, but this was the ultimate embarrassment for them.

But I had an intrinsic drive for more and that would not allow me to settle for the nothingness, dead-end I was being fed into my future. I set out to prove them wrong. The residual was a bar for success that had been set so high, I nearly killed myself to attain it. I wanted perfect grades. I wanted to look perfect at all times. I wanted the perfect boyfriend. I got the perfect grades. I looked perfect every day. But my perfection with choices of me was perfectly wrong. Instead of the "perfect" man, I got one who physically abused me. Another who mentally abused me and taunted me for being an unwed mother. He laughed at me at the suggestion that I was suitable for marriage. I even had one who devalued me to the point that date rape occurred. I was cheapened and felt worthless. You see, there is no perfection on this earth. I set myself up to a standard I could not reach. These choices and decisions were based on shame and doubt of who I was and what I was. I saw myself as imperfect. Therefore, I was not worthy of a love that did not include abuse in some form. I believed I wasn't good enough. So I chose relationships that punished me for having the desire and needing more.

I allowed envy, jealousy to seep into my life and hid behind their ugly masks. I used these as excuses for why I was not achieving or why someone else was achieving.

My relationships were promiscuous and unfulfilling. The culture of sexual freedom certainly did not do much to help either. As I reflected, I came to the intersection of two roads- the road I was on and the road where I wanted to be. The road I was on was not going to allow me to grow into the woman and mother I wanted to be. God saw fit to get me on track early. While in college, I was blessed with angels to poured light, love, and wisdom into me about success. They taught me about prayer but did not bang me over the head with a bible to do so. They did not condemn me for being an unwed mother. Again, I was a believer. But my depth of knowledge was so shallow and superficial. I attended church but did not attend to what the Bible taught me. The power of prayer rescued me from me. I wanted to blame my family. I wanted to blame the men I dated. Yes, my family was harsh but they were hurt. Yes, the men I dated were poor choices but they were my choices. Chosen because I didn't feel strong and capable. I needed someone else to play out the parent role, to pretend to keep me safe, protected me like a parent, and tell me "I love you." I thought this would be enough to complete me. I needed these voids filled in order to become whole.

My angels explained to me that I needed to take ownership of my situation and stop looking for someone to blame. I began to understand the danger if I stayed in the shadows of pain, fear, striving for perfection, sacrificing my body in hope of a brief reward of "I love you." If I did not step into the light, I would become addicted to the shadows. Those angels taught me that neither I nor any man could not complete me. The relationship I needed was with God. He alone would make me "complete" in order to align my goals and mission with His purpose. I needed that covenant relationship in order to grow. I was led to study "May the God of peace... make you complete in every good work to do His will through the blood of the everlasting covenant so you will be well pleasing in His sight, through Jesus Christ to whom be glory forever. (Heb. 13: 20-21)

These angels delivered me through conversations that were really lessons. They spoke to me in a language I understood- love, understanding, empathy, and sympathy.

Am I there yet? Well, my relationship with God has made me complete but I consider myself a work in progress in daily need of refinement. I cannot help but to wonder how much of this insecurity, lack of self-love and low self-esteem have I inadvertently passed on to my children? I have many conversations to have with them.

I have a husband whom I love dearly. I finally figured it out. I was involved in bad relationships because I was trying to problem solve the past, trying to change it instead of my response to it. I learned that I needed to choose a man who would challenge and support my growth. I learned I needed to mature and take ownership of my mind, body, energy, desires, dreams, actions and choices in life. I needed to look to God for guidance and direction, but ultimately the choice was mine to make.

I have found my way out of those shadows and now stand in the light of God. His light has allowed me growth and because I have trusted Him and entrusted my problems to Him in prayer, I have received the love I needed. I don't take my God for granted. Prayer is my direct phone line each day to call on God to direct and correct my daily walk.

The cliff of death taught me about life and how

precious it is and how prayer is the ultimate salve for the pain inflicted by death. In the span of four years, I planned 4 funerals. Twice I found myself involved in the decision to remove someone from life support.

I sat and watched the life take flight from my mother. One moment we sat laughing and talking, the next moment her head dropped to the side, she went into convulsions. I jumped up and began to shake her as she sat lifeless in the chair. Her big brown beautiful eyes seemed to look right past me, lifeless. I willed her back to me. But those few additional hours God granted were the best gift I could have had. I was able to say I love you, laugh with her a few more times before her final departure from me. When the doctors asked if they should continue to revive her, I prayed with my husband, I called my sister and we allowed Mom to go home. Her death came 36 days from the day we buried my stepfather. I was one year after we had buried my husband's younger brother. The night we laid my mother to rest, I was awakened by a voice telling me a scripture. I had to heed this voice, I had been there before. I reached for my bible and turned to Matthew 4:11 "Then the devil left him, and angels came and attended him." The sweetness of answered prayers, I knew the angels are with me.

Within a year, I had to say goodbye to my sister. It had been a long journey. I watched my beautiful sister become robbed of life, one day at a time over a span of eight years as she struggled with cancer. I prayed with her and for her. I was so arrogant with my faith that I sometimes became a useless tool for God and He spoke to me and corrected me. I was so fixated on how I thought she should pray that I lost sight of what God intended was for me. I was to be her prayer warrior but I was to also continue to learn about the power of prayer and ministry through prayer. We fought, we argued, we forgave, we loved one another. I cannot imagine what it is like to be told you have 6 months to live. My sister was angry. She had taken excellent care of herself. How could the doctors have missed this? She had always done things for those in need. Why was she being punished? I sought words to comfort her to no avail. I gave up. Then God spoke. He sent me to scriptures 3 times in one week. Each time awakening me in the wee hours of the morning. I would jot down the scripture and call my sister and tell her to read. One day I retrieved all my notes and read the scriptures. I had to cry. In each scripture was the word life! Hallelujah. Answered Prayers. Eight years were given and we used every precious minute.

Through each of these losses, I had to humble myself to God's will and remind myself of the words of The

Lord's Prayer- "Thy will be done on earth as it is in heaven." Thy will Lord, not mine. I prayed each time, "Heal my mother, my brother, my father, my sister if that is Thy will. Allow me to accept Your will no matter the outcome. Oh Lord embrace my mother, my sister, my brother, my father in Your love and usher them to Your kingdom. Send your angels to watch over me and help me through this grief. Yes, Lord, this bitter cup I must drink from knowing that you are here and that you have a plan that is greater than me." My prayer was not uttered in defeat, but in the victory. I was determined to rejoice, no matter what. And I did.

I had to surrender my power to God. Death pushed my boundaries of strength to new levels. Death allowed Him to mature me. What I once feared, I now embraced understood and accepted. This maturation allowed me to experience the stages of grief so effortlessly thanks to His

Holy Spirit. Yes, pain and loss remain constant visitors. But because I have surrendered to Christ through prayer, His grace and mercy allow their love for me and my love for them to flourish. I treasure each day and each life I have contact with.

Now, when I find myself standing on the edge of that cliff, I smile. What lies below is deep murky river filled tears and demons from my past. I am not afraid of my future. Through His grace and mercy, my wings of prayer have grown and allow me to get over because I let God!

AUTOBIOGRAPHY
for
Beatrice Moore

Beatrice Moore, The Lifestyle DIVVA, is an award-winning educator, author, and successful entrepreneur. As The Lifestyle DIVVA, she is an advocate for promoting and developing a positive lifestyle that rejects media representations of negativity and embraces the following principles: cultivate Determination to overcome life's trials; be an Inspiration and role model; cast a powerful Vision of and for yourself; acknowledge your Value, and; walk in faith, Assured that God is with you at all times!

She has used her gifts of teaching and leadership to support positive self-esteem and growth opportunities for educators nationally and internationally and now expands her reach of influence as The Lifestyle DIVVA.

In addition to authoring "How I Got Over-Prayers from a Woman on the Edge Who Let Go and Let God!" she is the author of the Shoe Fetish fiction novel series and co-founder of The Shoe Fetish Movement

Shoefetishmovement.com

1-888-321-9604

ABOUT THE AUTHOR

It's hard to sit on your talents, retreat from your destiny or settle for a less than optimized life when there's a spur in your side goading you to excellence. Memphis born LaTracey Copeland Hughes, also known as the Purposeful DIVA, has been that spur in the sides of countless audience members and readers of her dynamic recently released book. DIVA stands for Divinely Inspire Visionary Achiever, which describes this businesswoman and mother of four. Her book, "Just LaTracey: The Radical Christian Woman" debuted in November 2017. Through her works, she encourages and motivates others to excel, kick off shackles and live abundantly by overcoming adversity and casting off a faltered start.

Be it poverty or a catalog of layered challenges, she knows what it's like to persevere and overcome through resilience. When she teaches and writes about the Radical Christian woman; she is drawing from the wellspring of her own life.

She has risen from the ashes of what seemed to be defeat and destruction and emerged victorious and triumphant. Described as a gem in this season who has demonstrated that she's not easily broken, she has experienced success as CEO of the non-profit organization, Capstone Experience, Inc. She teaches others to do the same by thinking outside of the box, and using experiences as stepping stones to destiny and purpose.

"I want to leave my mark as a professional, virtuous example; in my home as a businesswoman and mother, and as a business consultant, speaker and author/publisher," she states.

LaTracey is not only modeling the examples she holds dear, but also teaching the virtuous lessons through the Radical Christian Woman Project. Her daily life serves to inspire others and her engaging presentations help people to envision greater outcomes. As a speaker, she provides her audiences with the essential elements that fuel her own vision of entrepreneurship, leadership, purpose-motivation, innovation and bravery.

LaTracey Copeland Hughes is available as a keynote speaker, workshop facilitator, in-house tailored speaker or for book signing events.

Audiences will hear how she trimmed away past hurts and pain to create passion, profit and purpose. She highlights the distractions that are keeping those from moving in their God-given Purpose. LaTracey will leave your audience with a sense of restoration in the areas needed most! She specializes in meeting women right where they are and supporting them not to stay Stuck On Purpose!

As an author, publisher and speaker who rose from very humble beginnings, She imparts a powerful message to woman's groups, non-profit organizations and schools. Her signature style is appropriate, real, raw, and unedited; while at the same time provoking thought and rich with clear points of value. She meets the needs and answers the heart-cry of her audiences.

For more information, or to book her for your ministry or woman's group, visit her website at www.purposefulpublishing.org